D0194489

THE
DINOSAURS
MEET
DR. CLOCK

by Martha Weston

Holiday House / New York

Library of Congress Cataloging-in-Publication Data
Weston, Martha.
The Dinosaurs Meet Dr. Clock / by Martha Weston.—1st ed.
p. cm.
Summary: Dr. Clock invents a time machine,
but his trip back to the era of the dinosaurs does not turn out
as he had expected.
ISBN 0-8234-1661-5 (hardcover)
[1. Time travel—Fiction. 2. Dinosaurs—Fiction.
3. Scientists—Fiction.] I. Title.
PZ7.W52645 Dr 2002
[E]—dc21   00-047190

To all the fine scientists
in my family,
with admiration
and love

"I did it!" says Dr. Clock.

"I made a time machine."

He takes a sandwich.

He takes important science stuff.

He is ready to go!

Dr. Clock sets the dials.

"Back to the dinosaurs!" he says.

He pushes the PAST button.

FFSSITT!

He is zipped back
to the time of the dinosaurs.

Dr. Clock opens the door.
The air is warm and wet.
Dr. Clock looks around.
A scientist watches
everything.

"Now I will find a dinosaur,"
says Dr. Clock.

"Aha!" he says. "Tracks!"

Dr. Clock finds a dinosaur.

Dr. Clock takes notes.
A scientist watches
everything.

"Hmm," he says.
"My dinosaur has horns.
   They are on his nose."

Dr. Clock finds another dinosaur.

"Hmm," he says.

"My dinosaur lives in a family."

It is hard for Dr. Clock
to take notes.

"Hmm," he says.

"My dinosaur eats only plants."

Dr. Clock is glad his dinosaur
eats only plants.

But Dr. Clock does not like
to eat swamp weeds.

He wants his sandwich.

All at once it is dark.
But it is not night.

"My dinosaurs are fast,"
Dr. Clock says.
"It's okay I do not have
my sandwich."

Dr. Clock feels floaty.

"Hmm," he says.

"Head butters? Of course!
Pachycephalosaurus!"
He says it like this:
pack-ee-sef-ah-lo-sore-us.

Dr. Clock cannot write
in his notebook.

Dr. Clock feels floaty again.

"A scientist
watches everything,"
says Dr. Clock.

"L-l-long b-b-bony b-b-back b-b-bone."

But it is hard to
watch dinosaurs.

Dr. Clock is not happy.

His notebook is gone.

His important science stuff is gone.

He is very hungry.

And where is the time machine?

"Pull yourself together, Clock!"
he says.

Dr. Clock sees some tracks.
"I remember these!" he says.
He follows them.

He sees the dinosaurs' nest.
He sees ferns.
Dr. Clock tiptoes by.

Now he sees some other tracks.
He follows them.

Here is his important science stuff.
Here is his sandwich.

And here is his time machine!

Before you can say
"pack-ee-sef-ah-lo-sore-us,"
Dr. Clock is setting dials.

"To the lab!" says Dr. Clock.
He pushes the FUTURE button.

FFSSITT!

He is zipped forward in time.

Dr. Clock opens the door.

"Oops," he says.

"This is not my lab."

He is right.

He did not watch the dials.

A scientist watches everything.

At least this time
he has his sandwich.